AF316815

Bloomy

Written By
Elizabeth Minotti

Illustrated By
Kidsbook Art LLC

First Edition

Issued in print and electronic formats
(Hardcover) ISBN: 978-969-50-9238-5
(Electronic) ISBN: 978-969-50-9237-8

DARK SWAN
PUBLISHING

To Liam,
my sunshine

Sometimes I feel sunny
like a buttercup

Sometimes I feel cozy
like a pussy willow

sometimes I feel gutsy
like a dandelion

Sometimes I feel prickly
like a cactus

Sometimes I feel friendly
like a wildflower

Sometimes I feel topsy-turvy
like an ivy

Sometimes I feel teeny-tiny
like an acorn

Sometimes I feel mighty
like an oak tree

Sometimes I feel dreamy
like a rose

Sometimes I feel funny, jumpy, bubbly, silly, itchy, pokey, grumbly, sleepy, smelly, and snuggly...

Just like me!

Bloomy Facts!

- A buttercup's bowl shaped petals reflect yellow light. If you hold a buttercup under your chin and there is a yellow reflection on your skin, that means you like butter!

- The soft, silky silvery puffs on a pussy willow are called catkins and feel like real fur.

- Dandelions are adventurous and bold flowers that can grow anywhere. When they are ready to seed, they turn from golden yellow into beautiful white globes of fluff. Each seed fluff can be carried miles away on the wind! Some believe that the seeds are wishes, and if you blow the seeds into the air your wishes will come true! Others say that dandelion seeds are your thoughts and dreams and blowing them will carry them to the ones you love.

- Cacti have been on Earth since the dinosaurs and can go months without any water!

- Ivy can climb up walls and trees, and can grow to almost a hundred feet high!

- Acorns grow from oaks, and only 1 in 10,000 acorns will actually become a tree!

- Oak trees can live to be a thousand years old!

- Roses have been treasured for thousands of years for their dramatic beauty and fragrance. They have been found in the pyramids, appear in ancient Greek and Roman myths, and is a favorite of poets and authors. Archaeologists found fossilized roses over 40 million years old!